My "b" Sound Box®

WITHDRAWN

WRITTEN BY JANE BELK MONCURE • ILLUSTRATED BY REBECCA THORNBURGH

Published by The Child's World®
1980 Lookout Drive • Mankato, MN 56003-1705
800-599-READ • www.childsworld.com

ISBN HARDCOVER: 9781503823051
ISBN PAPERBACK: 9781503831278
LCCN: 2017960281

Printed in the United States of America
PA02371

A NOTE TO PARENTS AND EDUCATORS:

Magic moon machines and five fat frogs are just a few of the fun things you can share with children by reading books with them. Reading aloud helps children in so many ways! It introduces them to new words, motivates them to develop their own reading skills, and expands their attention span and listening abilities. So it's important to find time each day to share a book or two . . . or three!

As you read with young children, you can help develop their understanding of how print works by talking about the parts of the book—the cover, the title, the illustrations, and the words that tell the story. As you read, use your finger to point to each word, modeling a gentle sweep from left to right.

Simple word games help develop important prereading skills, including an understanding of rhyme and alliteration (when words share the same beginning sound, such as "six" and "sand"). Try playing with words from a book you've just shared: "What other words start with the same sound as moon?" "Cat and hat, do those words rhyme?" The possibilities are endless—and so are the rewards!

My "b" Sound Box®

Little  had a box. "I will find things that begin with my **b** sound," she said.

"I will put them into my sound box."

Little  put on her bonnet and went for a walk.

Little  found a bird and a birdbath.

Did she put the bird and the birdbath in the box? She did.

Little  found a bunny.

Did she put the bunny into the box with  the bird and the birdbath? She did.

Then Little heard a sound.

"Buzzzzzz." It was a bee.

She put the bee into the box, carefully!

Next, she found a baby baboon in a tree.

The baby baboon was eating a banana.

"I will put you into my box," said Little ![b].

 The box was so big she could hardly carry it.

She found a bicycle with a basket on the back.

She put the box into the basket and

rode the bicycle over a big bump!

The baby baboon, the bunny, and

the bird bounced out of the box.

Little  bounced off the bicycle.

"That was a bad bump!" she said.

Then she saw a ball and a bat. "Let's play ball!" she said. And they did.

The baby baboon hit the ball with the bat. The ball bounced into a bush.

Something was behind the bush. It was a bear. He
gave the ball to Little . "Thank you, Bear," she said.

She put the bear, the bush, and the ball into the

box. She put the baby baboon, the bat, the bird,

the birdbath, and the bunny back, too.

The bee said, "Buzz, buzz, this box might break!"

"I must find something bigger," said Little.

She rode her bicycle over a bridge.

Under the bridge, she saw a boat, a big, big boat.

She jumped into the boat and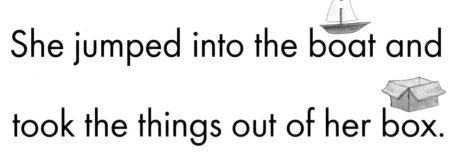

took the things out of her box.

"This is big enough," she said.

"Big enough for all of us."

And it was!

Little 's Word List

baboon

bee

box

ball

bicycle

bridge

banana

bird

bump

basket

birdbath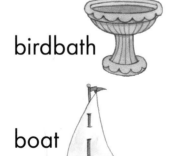

bunny

bat

boat

bush

bear

bonnet

Other Words with Little

bag

bed

bottle

balloon

bell

bowl

barn

belt

brush

basketball

bone

bug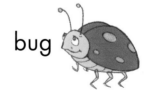

bathtub

book

butterfly

More to Do!

Little  had quite an adventure when she put on her bonnet! You can play a fun game with things that begin with the letter **b**.

Directions:

Begin by sitting in a circle with your friends. Have one person hold a small ball. This person is the first player. The first player says:

> I was on my bike.
> Then I hit a bump...
> A big, big bump!
> And into my basket bounced a _____.
> (Here the player names something that starts with a **b** sound.)

The first player now passes the ball to the person sitting to the right. The new player repeats the rhyme. He or she must include the **b** object that the first player said, and add a new **b** object. Each player repeats the rhyme, naming all the things that have been said and adding one more **b** object. See how long you can keep the game going!

Here are a few words to get you started:

backpack	bead	biscuit	bowl
badger	bean	bobcat	bracelet
banjo	berry	boot	button

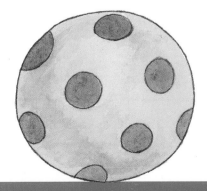

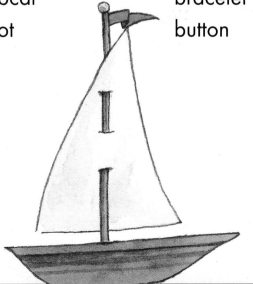

About the Author

Best-selling author Jane Belk Moncure (1926–2013) wrote more than 300 books throughout her teaching and writing career. After earning a master's degree in early childhood education from Columbia University, she became one of the pioneers in that field. In 1956, she helped form the Virginia Association for Early Childhood Education, which established the first statewide standards for teachers of young children.

    Inspired by her work in the classroom, Mrs. Moncure's books became standards in primary education, and her name was recognized across the country. Her success was reflected not only in her books' popularity with parents, children, and educators, but also by numerous awards, including the 1984 C. S. Lewis Gold Medal Award.

About the Illustrator

Rebecca Thornburgh lives in a pleasantly spooky old house in Philadelphia. If she's not at her drawing table, she's reading—or singing with her band, called Reckless Amateurs. Rebecca has one husband, two daughters, and two silly dogs.